Disney's
THE HUNCHBACK
OF NOTRE DAME

© 1996 Disney Enterprises, Inc.

GOLDEN BOOKS & DESIGN,™ A GOLDEN BOOK,® and
the distinctive gold spine are trademarks of Western Publishing Company, Inc.

A GOLDEN BOOK®
Western Publishing Company, Inc.
Racine, Wisconsin 53404
No part of this book may be reproduced or copied in any form without
written permission from the copyright owner. Produced in U.S.A.

QUASIMODO

FROLLO

HUGO

VICTOR

LAVERNE

ACHILLES

GARGOYLE
FUN

GARGOYLES MATCH—
BUT WATCH OUT FOR FROLLO!
(A card game for 2)

Color and cut out the cards on this page and the next. Deal
all the cards. Players place any pairs they have face-up in front
of them. Then players take turns drawing a card from each
other's hand—trying not to get Frollo. If a pair is formed, the
two cards are laid down face-up. When all pairs have been made,
the player left with the Frollo card loses.

LAVERNE

© Disney

VICTOR

© Disney

LAVERNE

© Disney

VICTOR

© Disney

FROLLO

© Disney

LAVERNE

© Disney

LAVERNE

© Disney

VICTOR

© Disney

VICTOR

© Disney

DRAW HUGO
Use the picture as a guide.

MAKE A HUGO MASK

1. Tear out this page and decorate the mask.
2. Glue the page to lightweight cardboard.
3. Cut out the mask and the eyeholes.
4. Punch holes through the dots on the sides. Thread yarn or string through each hole and knot it. Fit to your head, and tie in the back.

Design your own gargoyle mask.
Follow the directions for the Hugo mask.

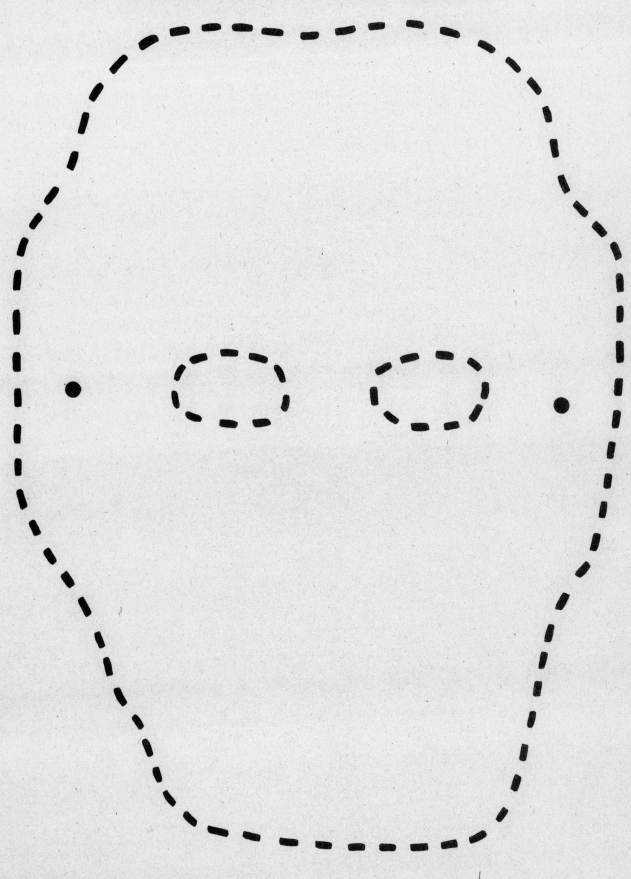

What is Laverne saying to the pigeons?

Use the number code to find out.

1 = U 2 = M 3 = G 4 = O 5 = E 6 = R 7 = I

8 = Y 9 = D 10 = T 11 = V 12 = N 13 = A

MESSAGE:

DON'T YOU EVER
9 4 12 10 8 4 1 5 11 5 6

MIGRATE?
2 7 3 6 13 10 5

ANSWER: DON'T YOU EVER MIGRATE?

Find the pigeons hiding in the picture.

Get Quasimodo to the Festival of Fools.

**Design your own Festival of Fools banners.
Use the designs in the border for ideas.**

TOPSY-TURVY WORD SEARCH

At the Festival of Fools, everything is TOPSY-TURVY! Look up, down, forward, backward, and diagonally to find the crazy words in the puzzle below. Use the word list for help.

ABSURD	GAGA	SILLY
BONKERS	INSANE	TOPSY-TURVY
CRAZY	INSIDE OUT	UPSIDE DOWN
FLIPPED OUT	LUNACY	UPSY-DAISY
FOOLISH	NUTTY	WACKY

```
L  Y  S  I  A  D  Y  S  P  U  C  T
L  Y  E  V  R  U  T  Y  S  P  Y  I  O
Y  Z  N  Y  L  L  I  S  S  B  K  N  P
Z  A  A  F  O  O  L  I  S  H  C  S  S
A  R  S  T  C  U  D  P  H  K  A  I  Y
R  C  N  O  W  E  Z  A  M  G  W  D  T
C  B  I  R  D  Y  J  Q  G  L  E  E  U
B  G  B  O  N  K  E  R  S  A  V  O  R
G  I  W  F  Y  C  A  N  U  L  G  U  V
I  N  F  L  I  P  P  E  D  O  U  T  Y
N  N  U  T  T  Y  D  R  U  S  B  A  O
```

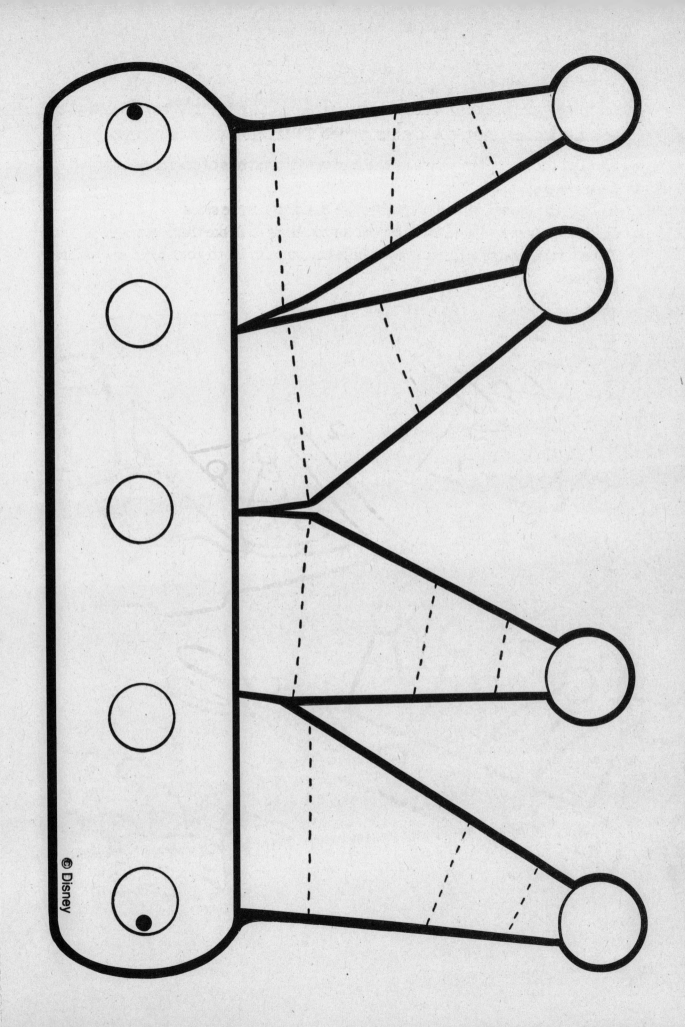

© Disney

MAKE PUPPETS AND A STAGE

You'll need safety scissors, crayons or markers, non-toxic glue, tape, lightweight cardboard, a cereal box, paper, and pencils or wooden craft sticks.

1. Carefully tear the next two pages from the book and decorate the pictures.
2. Glue the pages to cardboard.
3. Cut out the puppets and decorations.
4. Tape a pencil or craft stick to the back of each puppet.
5. To make a stage, cut the back and top from a cereal box. Cut a large window in the top front of the box (be sure to leave a border around the window). Glue the decorations at the top and sides of the window. Cover the rest of the stage front with paper. You may need to set a small book or other object on the bottom flap of your stage to make it stand better.
6. Now, put on a show with your puppets and stage!

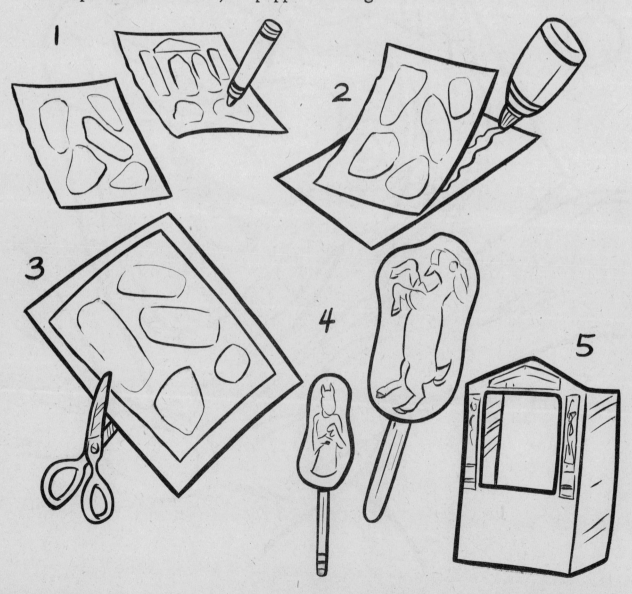

© Disney

© Disney

© Disney

© Disney

© Disney

MAKE A TAMBOURINE

You'll need 2 paper plates, crayons or markers, tape, a paper punch, 8 small jingle bells, and ribbon or yarn.

1. Decorate the bottoms of the plates.
2. With the decorated bottoms facing out, tape the plate edges together in a few places.
3. Punch a hole for each bell around the edge of the plates. Punch a few extra holes for streamers.
4. Thread string through the bell holes and the bells, and tie. Thread yarn or ribbon for streamers through the extra holes, and tie.

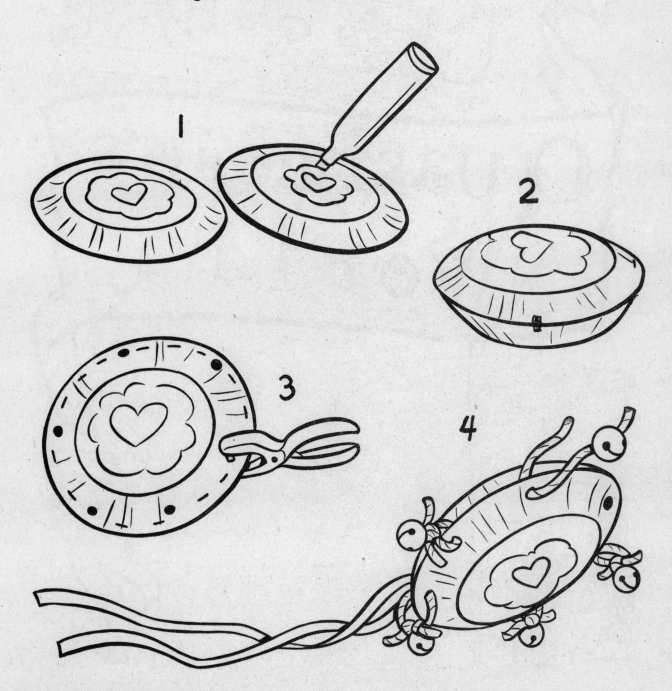

What does Quasimodo tell the baby bird?
Use the symbol code to find out.
Write the letters on the lines.

A	B	C	D	E	F	G	H	I	J	K	L	M
▲	★	✿	◗	✖	✳	❄	♥	◯	✸	♦	❣	◆

N	O	P	Q	R	S	T	U	V	W	X	Y	Z
◆	●	✿	✪	■	✦	✳	▼	▮	✸	✦	✔	★

N O B O D Y
◆ ● ★ ● ◗ ✔

S H O U L D
✦ ♥ ● ▼ ❣ ◗

S T A Y
✦ ✳ ▲ ✔

C O O P E D
✿ ● ● ✿ ✖ ◗

U P H E R E
▼ ✿ ♥ ✖ ■ ✖

F O R E V E R
✳ ● ■ ✖ ▮ ✖ ■

ANSWER: NOBODY SHOULD STAY COOPED UP HERE FOREVER.

How many times can you find the name QUASIMODO in the puzzle below?
(Hint: Look down and diagonally!)

```
Q Q Q Q Q Q Q Q Q
U U U U U U U U U
A A A A A A A A A
S S S S S S S S S
I I I I I I I I I
M M M M M M M M M
O O O O O O O O O
D D D D D D D D D
O O O O O O O O O
```

ANSWER: 9 TIMES DOWN, 2 TIMES DIAGONALLY

Frollo says he is Quasimodo's
friend and protector,
but he is really the opposite.
Draw lines to match these opposites.

1. KIND   A. BAD
2. LOVE   B. HARSH
3. GENEROUS   C. CRUEL
4. PROTECT   D. ENEMY
5. GOOD   E. STINGY
6. FRIEND   F. HATE
7. GENTLE   G. DESTROY

ANSWERS: 1-C, 2-F, 3-E, 4-G, 5-A, 6-D, 7-B

What is Phoebus saying to Quasimodo?
Use Quasimodo's code to find out.

A = ♠
G = (shape)
M = (jester)
S = (crown)
Y = (hook)

B = (shape)
H = (shape)
N = (shape)
T = (circle)
Z = (clover)

C = ♦
I = (cap)
O = ♥
U = ♣

D = (mask)
J = (horn)
P = ◇
V = (mask)

E = ✤
K = ◇
Q = (shape)
W = (shape)

F = ✤
L = (eyes)
R = (shape)
X = (shape)

MESSAGE:

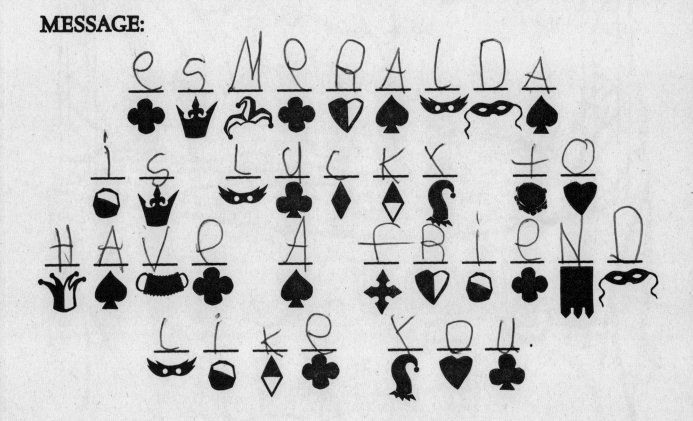

DRAW DJALI
Use the picture as a guide.

Djali is hungry.

Help him find something to munch.

Djali isn't *just* jolly – he has lots of different feelings.

Under each word, write how Djali looks.
Use the following words for help:
angry, happy, loving, surprised, worried, scared.

_____

_____

_____

_____

_____

_____